Animal Homes

Betsey Chessen • Pamela Chanko

Scholastic Inc.
New York • Toronto • London • Auckland • Sydney

Acknowledgments

Science Consultants: Patrick R. Thomas, Ph.D., Bronx Zoo/Wildlife Conservation Park; Glenn Phillips, The New York Botanical Garden; **Literacy Specialist:** Maria Utefsky, Reading Recovery Coordinator, District 2, New York City

Design: MKR Design, Inc.

Photo Research: Barbara Scott

Endnotes: Susan Russell

Photographs: *Cover:* Tim Davis/Photo Researchers, Inc.; p. 1: Dwight Kuhn; p. 2: Robert & Linda Mitchell; p. 3: John Gerlach/DRK Photo; p. 4: D. Cavagnaro/DRK Photo; p. 5: John Cancalosi; p. 6: Michael Francis/The Wildlife Collection; p. 7: Harry Rogers/Photo Researchers, Inc.; p. 8: Steven C. Kaufman/DRK Photo; p. 9: Tom & Pat Leeson/DRK Photo; p. 10: C. Allan Morgan/ Peter Arnold, Inc.; p. 11: Tim Davis/ Photo Researchers, Inc.; p. 12: Robert & Linda Mitchell.

Library of Congress Cataloging-in-Publication Data
Chessen, Betsey 1970-
Animal homes / Betsey Chessen, Pamela Chanko.
p. cm. -- (Science emergent readers)
"Scholastic early childhood."
Includes index.
Summary: Photographs and simple text describe the habitats of different animals.
ISBN 0-590-76166-8 (pbk.: alk.paper)
1. Animals--Habitations--Juvenile literature. [1. Animals--Habitations.]
I. Chanko, Pamela, 1968-. II. Title. III. Series.
QL756.C486 1998
591.56'4--dc21   97-29186
                                                                                      CIP AC

9   10   03   02   01   00

A log is a home for a squirrel.

A nest is a home for birds.

A cave is a home for bats.

A web is a home for a spider.

A tunnel is a home for a mouse.

A den is a home for raccoons.

A hive is a home for bees.

A lodge is a home for a beaver.

A swamp is a home for an alligator.

A burrow is a home for a prairie dog.

A tree is a home for chimpanzees.

And a shell is a home for a hermit crab.

Next to man, the Beaver (left) builds the most complex home. Inside what looks like a mound of sticks in a pond is a dry and cozy place to raise a family. The Alligator (right) uses the whole swamp for a home, cruising almost unseen as it hunts.

Prairie Dogs (left) create whole towns. Their burrows connect to make complicated underground homes and systems for escape. Like most primates, the Chimpanzees (right) make very simple nests in trees to sleep in at night. They use branches and big jungle leaves. Often they move on to a new tree for the next night.

The Hermit Crab (right) adopts its home, borrowing an empty shell for protection. It will move to a new shell home when it outgrows the old one.

Animal Homes

Animal homes are built for different purposes. Mammals construct homes, which they usually live in alone or in single family units, to serve as places for protection. Birds build homes when it's time to nest and raise a family. The animal and bird homes in these

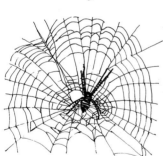

pages reflect the many ways shelters are built and used. The Blue Jay (left) builds a nest once a year when it's time to lay eggs. The Mexican Freetail Bats (right) make their homes hanging upside down in caves. Here they can hibernate for seven cold months.

The Banded Garden Spider (left) builds what is called an "orb" web. This home is used for trapping prey. The Desert Pocket Mouse (right) makes tunnels in the sand for protection from heat and predators.

These baby Raccoons (left) stay at home in their burrow in the ground to wait for their mother to bring back food. The Honeybee hive (right) is an elaborate effort by many bee builders and acts as both a home and a warehouse for storing pollen and honey.